DC Comics

Batman created by Bob Kane

BATMAN & DRACULA: RED RAIN

DC Comics, 1700 Broadway, New York, NY 10019
A division of Warner Bros. - A Time Warner Entertainment Company
Printed in Canada. Sixth Printing
ISBN: 1-56389-036-4

Cover illustrations by Kelley Jones and Malcolm Jones III

BATMAN & DRACULA

red rain

DOUG MOENCH
WRITER

KELLEY JONES
PENCILLER

MALCOLM JONES III
INKER

LES DORSCHEID
COLORIST

TODD KLEIN
LETTERER

Thanks to Bob Kane, Bill Finger, Bram Stoker, and Hammer for inspiration; Kelley and Malcolm for brilliant work; Winnie, Gil, Pam, Deb, and Derek just because; and Denny O'Neil for tossing a dart at the menu. —DM

Thanks to Carl Laemmle, Jr., Samuel Arkoff, Anthony Keys, Terence Fisher, Freddy Francis, Philip Martel. —KJ

Thanks to Doug Moench, Kelley Jones, Kelley Puckett, Denny O'Neil, Kevin Dooley, Randy DuBurke, Keith Giffen, Dick Giordano, Pat Bastienne, Paul Levitz, Ruthie Thomas, Tamara Painter, and Juliette Palmer. —MJ

Wasn't it Prince who wrote, "I've seen the future and it works"? Sure. Maybe he was talking about *this* particular alternate future, mind-numbingly frightening and just around that closest dark corner.

I've never been a fan of cross-referencing characters from different milieus, principally because whether you mean it or not, the result too often resembles *Abbott & Costello Meet the Mummy.* So it was with a good degree of trepidation that I agreed to take a first look at *RED RAIN,* this Batman/Dracula cross-pollination.

I'm not ashamed to say I was hooked from the first panel. And why not? Doug Moench's script and Messrs. Jones' art have given us an altogether different Batman than we're used to—and all the while keeping within the moral and intellectual boundaries that define the Batman's inner world.

It always seemed to me that because Batman spoke to us from under cover of the night, he addressed our most primitive emotions. We didn't have to *think* about Batman, we only had to *feel.* About a third of the way through this story it struck me that this had been my precise reaction to Bram Stoker's brilliant novel, *Dracula.*

And, for as long as I have been reading Batman, I have always wondered if this mythical character—so powerful, so charismatic, so erotic—played a role in the creation of Batman. For, after all, though Batman is—and always has been—a champion of justice, his has been a cruel justice, one of fear, intimidation and dark vengeance. Bruce Wayne's original mandate was nothing less than to strike terror in the hearts of all criminals.

We may as well admit it. What has made Batman such an utterly compelling hero is his power, charisma and eroticism. It seems natural, then, that he inhabit this scarifying moment in time in Dracula's alternate future.

Gotham City seems ripe for the lord of vampires, doesn't it? The dark, grimy urban swamp has become a nightmare world so like many of our post-modern urban landscapes, inhabited by shambling *untermenschen,* seemingly irredeemably decayed.

The lights have gone out, and there's nothing left but darkness. Batman, dweller in the dark, was created to be, first and foremost, a detective. His first assignment—overt or not, conscious or not—was to find the murderer of his parents. But he was no detective in the classical mold. While the other great detectives of literature, such as Sherlock Holmes or Nero Wolfe, lived more or less on a purely intellectual plane, or were strictly hard guys, like Philip Marlowe and the Continental Op, Batman's character is a potent alloy of the deductive mind dispensing primitive Justice.

And this flux of the deductive and the visceral is what *RED RAIN* has captured so well. To take two such dynamic characters from such utterly different milieus and make their encounter meaningful as well as exciting is no mean feat. What *RED RAIN* is *not* is two entities duking it out for forty-two pages. *That* kind of story I can do without, having read through ten thousand of them over the years. No, *RED RAIN* has more on its mind than hand-to-hand combat. And, oddly enough, its relevance today is greater than it might have been even two years ago. Here is the beginning of the end of our dreams.

Death, destruction and the night. Who better to play out this final drama upon such a perfectly sordid stage than Dracula and Batman? And who could foretell the shocking finale of that drama? Certainly not me. And, I'll wager, you won't, either.

Never has Batman seemed more human. Never has he appeared so profoundly the iron-willed guardian of our dreams and hopes, the night-black avenger of our hurts and fears. Here, presented for your pleasure, is an alternate reality that is certain to shock as well as entertain.

As Prince wrote, "I've seen the future and, boy, it's rough."

—Eric V. Lustbader

THE RED RAINS DO NOT CEASE UNTIL WELL PAST MIDNIGHT...
...AND THOSE WHO EMERGE TO STRUT AND SLINK THROUGH THE SHADOWY VAPORS ARE FEW...
SLUMMIN' ON THE OLD BOP-HOP, FRIEND?
AH... PARDON ME?

I MEAN, YOU'RE SHOPPIN' FOR KICKS, RIGHT?
I AM... RECENTLY ARRIVED.
FROM EUROPE.
WHOA.

LUCKY ME--A POOR CHICK FROM CLEVELAND...
...FACIN' A CONTINENTAL BOP ON HOPP STREET.
COME BACK HERE.
SOMEBODY JUST JUNKED A COUCH AND THEY DON'T PICK UP TILL TUESDAY.

Y'KNOW, I DON'T USUALLY ASK FOR MONEY, BUT, LIKE, IF YOU COULD HELP ME WITH--
SILENCE.

WH--?
I DON'T GIVE.
I TAKE.

VACANCIES AVAILABLE

SHRRREP

"BOP... HOP."

Number two.

WAYNE MANOR: DUSK OF THE FOLLOWING DAY...

It starts as a mist, sinuous, hypnotic...

...and ends as woman.

I... can't move.
Spellbound.

Her eyes... fill me... pinning me...

Suddenly she's close...

...fluttering softly above... a presence of scent and movement, slow and fast...

Warm breath and murmured words...
...something about the night... eternal darkness... and a gift...

Then... spiralling blackness...
...veiled in shifting red mist.

HIIIHH
Gone--woman and mist...

Nothing-- just a dream...
...brought on by the girl off Hopp Street, her throat slashed on a couch under no roof...

SUN'S WAKIN' UP CHINA, TIME TO SHUT DOWN HERE...

Night.
Time to rise...

NINE O'CLOCK AN' ALL'S HELL...
GOTHAM GAZETTE

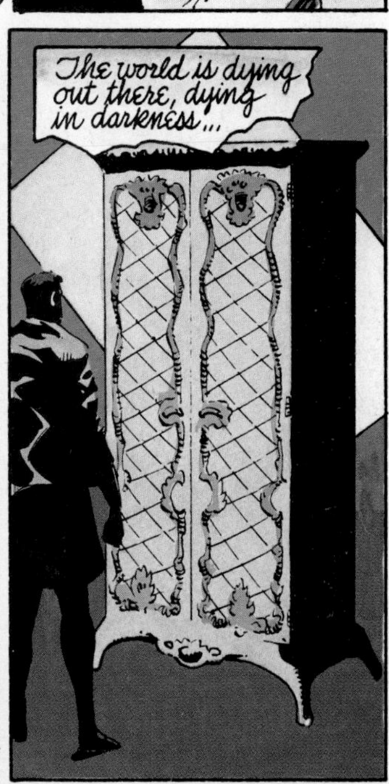
The world is dying out there, dying in darkness...

C'MON, YOU!
THIS AIN'T NO PLACE TO SPEND THE NIGHT.
YEAH--NOT EVEN ONE DECENT CLOSET...

...BUT THE DAMN SAVOY WENT AN' BOOKED ITSELF SOLID.
ALL RIGHT, COMEDIAN, BUT YOU DON'T WANNA SLEEP HERE.
SURE DON'T--
--BUT LAST NIGHT ONE O' YOUR COLLEAGUES JACKED ME OUTTA THE BUS TERMINAL...
"INTERRUPTED A VERY WILD DREAM, TOO..."

TONIGHT I FIGURE I'LL SKIP THE RUMPUS.
DANGEROUS OUT HERE, FOOL.
ONLY IF YOU GOT SOMETHIN' THEY WANT...

"...ONLY IF YOU'RE WORTH HUNTIN'."

AHH, SUIT YOURSELF.
HEY, MAN, I GOT NOTHIN' NOBODY'D WANT.

NOTHIN', OLD MAN...
HUH?
WHO SAID THAT--?

...'CEPT JUICE-SPIKED BLOOD.
NYAAAHHRRRRR
Below.
In that alley...
...but too late.
Again.
And this makes the third now...
Gotham Gazette
Mayor announces 2nd term bid
The third throat ripped to its death rattle...
...and still nothing in the news.

--NINETEEN THROAT-SLASHINGS THUS FAR, MAYOR WOODS, AND--
MORE, GORDON--AND STILL COUNTING.
WHAT--?
THERE ARE VICTIMS EVEN I DON'T KNOW ABOUT? AND YOU WANT TO--
DO YOU REALIZE WHAT COULD HAPPEN TO ME--GOTHAM'S FIRST BLACK MAYOR--IF PEOPLE START BELIEVING I CAN'T EVEN PROTECT THE DISENFRANCHISED OF MY OWN CITY?
IN WHICH CASE, MAYBE WE SHOULD DO SOMETHING TO PROTECT THEM, INSTEAD OF SWEEPING IT UNDER THE RUG AND COVERING UP ASPECTS OF IT FROM THE POLICE COMMISSIONER HIMSEL--

COMMISSIONER GORDON, I AM ORDERING YOU TO DO SOMETHING ABOUT IT!
I AM ORDERING YOU TO FIND AND STOP THIS HOMICIDAL MANIAC--WHILE I GO ABOUT THE BUSINESS OF MAINTAINING ORDER AND CALM IN THIS CITY!
LET ME GET THIS STRAIGHT.
YOU WANT A FULL-SCALE INVESTIGATION... BUT IT'S GOT TO BE KEPT LOW-KEY AND OUT OF THE MEDIA.
COMMISSIONER GORDON...
VERY WELL, MR. MAYOR.

I'LL DO EVERYTHING I CAN--
--WITHOUT SEEMING TO DO ANYTHING.

The dream again... beauty blossoming from mist...
...or is it a dream?

Can you dream the state of dreaming...?
And if you do... does that make it real?

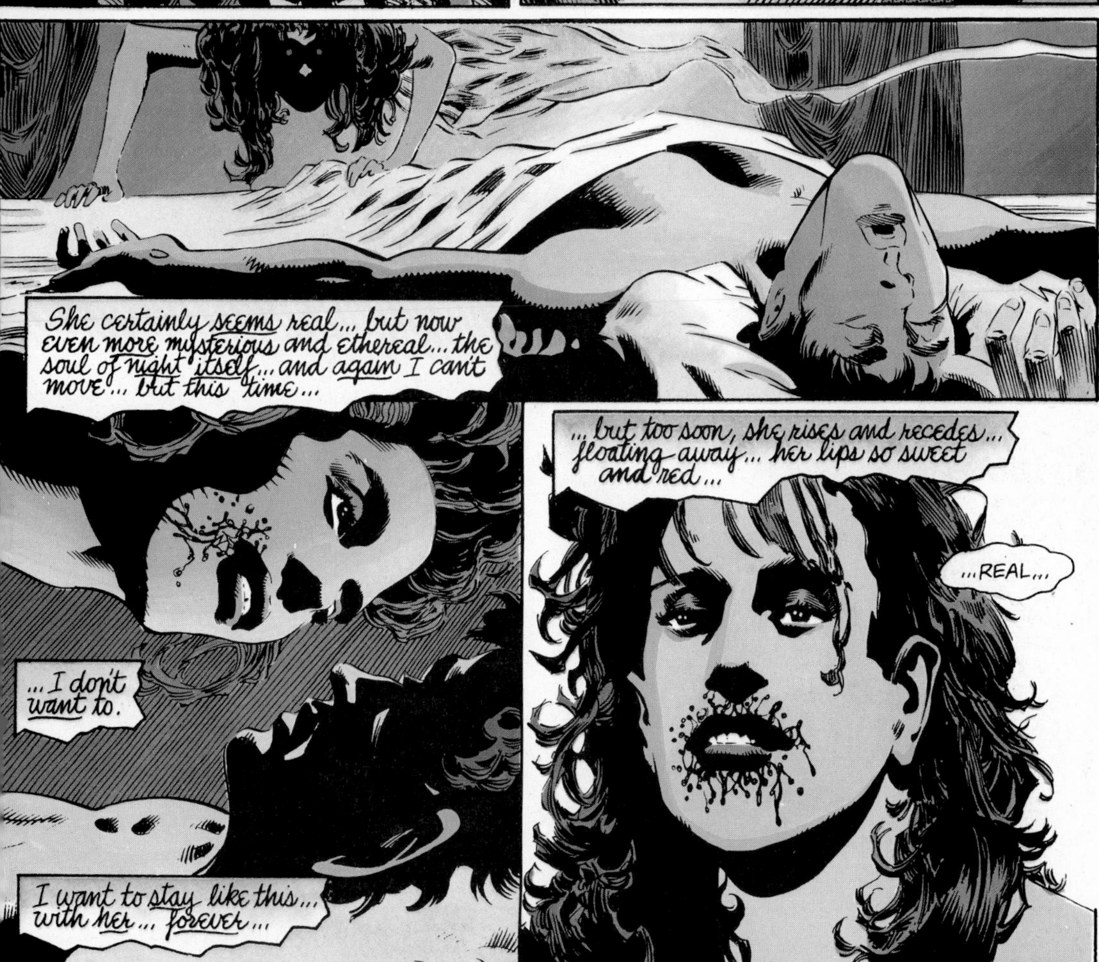
She certainly seems real... but now even more mysterious and ethereal... the soul of night itself... and again I can't move... but this time...
...I don't want to.
I want to stay like this... with her... forever...
...but too soon, she rises and recedes... floating away... her lips so sweet and red...
...REAL...

...WE'RE... REALLL...

awake -- refreshed, vibrant.
It's late again...
...and this night is special ...a pungent darkness of thrilling wind.
It's always been my element, the night...
...but somehow I've never felt closer to it, more at home in its rough endless folds.

It's as if the dream has empowered me... as if the soul of night herself has merged with my own soul...
...making of me a shred of darkness come to life.
But there's death in this darknes too, and all three victims were street people, homeless and hopeless... the type found too abundantly--

--in the twisting mazes and warrens of Greyfields.
KREEK
REEK

HSSSSS
KREEK
REEK
CAT--?

RAHRRR!
EEEEEEE

WAKK
UHN--!

REHRRRAHRRR
Yes...

...in Greyfields...
SWUDD
...but I never expected a woman.
She's clearly mad, almost demonic in her mask of blood spurted from the slashed throat...
...but this time I've caught her.
This time I'm not minutes or moments too late.
This time she's--
HSSSSS
What--?
So fast...
SHREPT

SWAKT
SHUMP
FRAK!
KRUNK!
It... can't be...
Even on uppers or devil-dust, no woman of her size should be that powerful... stronger than anyone I've ever faced...
Got to stop her--in that courtyard...
But...
WHERE...?

YEAH, BUT WHEN HE KEEPS HITTIN' ON BUMS LIKE THIS, WHO'S COUNTIN'?

Then again, mayb the press won't even notice, or care. Maybe they' all be off chasin sex scandals or the new slim Elvis on Oprah.

WELCOME HOME, SIR.
I THOUGHT IT BEST TO MEET YOU DOWN HERE AND REVIEW YOUR UP-COMING SLATE OF BRUCE WAYNE OBLIGATIONS...

WEDNESDAY NOON IS THE CHARITY LUNCHEON AT THE CIVIC CENTER.
THURSDAY MORNING YOU HAVE A MEETING WITH THE FINANCE DIRECTOR OF--
CANCEL THEM ALL.

SIR--?
I'M BUSY, ALFRED...

...AND I'M TIRED--VERY TIRED.
I don't like lying to him, not to Alfred, of all people...

But how can I tell him that the real reason is...daylight...
...and the unbearable prospect of going out in it?

How can I tell him that for all intents and purposes... Bruce Wayne is dead...
...and it's only the night now, only the dark side, that holds any meaning?

Night again... time to rise...
But I think...

...I'm still asleep...
...still...dreaming...
...REAL...
...VAMPIRES... ARE REAL...
...BUT NOT ALL OF THEM... EVIL.

Awake again.
And gone again.

But this time it was more than a dream...
...and something happened.

Yes--my back.
It seems Bruce Wayne was buried prematurely--and it's time for him to rise again...

...if only in the night, and if only to--
SPRAKT

The door handle--?

Locked--the door was locked...
And I simply tried to... open it.

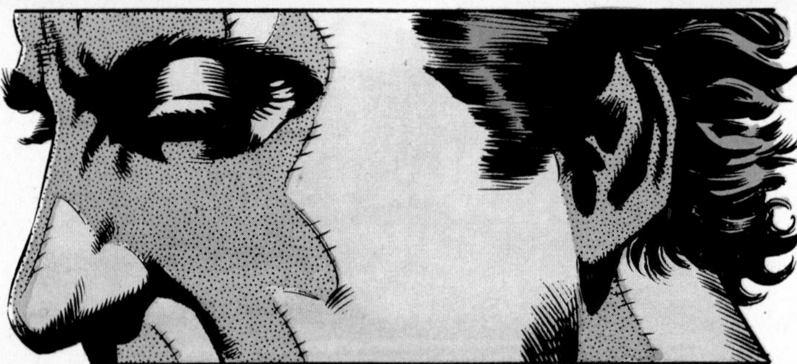
No effort, no strain.
What is... happening to me?

--MIGHT HELP, BRUCE, IF YOU AT LEAST TOLD ME WHAT I'M SUPPOSED TO BE LOOKING FOR IN THE BLOOD.
IF I KNEW THAT, DR. CHURCH, I WOULDN'T NEED YOUR HELP.

JUST CHECK FOR... ANYTHING UNUSUAL.
"UNUSUAL."

LIKE COMING TO MY HOME IN THE NIGHT FOR AN IMPROMPTU EXAM AFTER MISSING YOUR LAST THREE REGULAR PHYSICALS.
UNUSUAL LIKE THAT?

JUST CHECK, DOCTOR.

HMMM...
WELL, WE'LL NEED FULL RESULTS FROM THE LAB TESTS, OF COURSE, BUT RIGHT NOW I DON'T SEE ANYTHING... "UNUSUAL."

VERY WELL.
NOW TAKE A LOOK AT MY BACK-- MY SHOULDER BLADES.
EH--?
HAVE YOU... SCRAPED OR FALLEN ON YOUR BACK RECENTLY?

NO... NO, THAT'S NOT IT.
WHAT DO YOU SEE?
CONTUSIONS, I SHOULD SAY...
DO YOU WANT TO TELL ME WHAT'S GOING ON, BRUCE?

JUST HAVE THAT BLOOD TESTED, DOCTOR, AND GET BACK TO ME WITH THE RESULTS.
UH, TELL ME, BRUCE... HAVE YOU, AH, BEEN PUSHING YOURSELF LATELY?

NO, DR. CHURCH, I HAVEN'T.
BUT I'M ABOUT TO START.

WE BROUGHT YOU THE BEST, MASTER, JUST LIKE YOU SAID...
RUNAWAYS FRESH OUT OF THE BUS TERMINAL.

ARE ANY OF THEM ON DRUGS?

NO, MASTER-- WE CHECKED 'EM EVERY INCH.
NO NEEDLE MARKS ANYWHERE!
THEN BRING THEM...

...CLOSER.

I NEED INFORMATION, ARIANE...
...ABOUT VAMPIRE LORE.
THOUGHT I FELT A DRAFT IN HERE--CANDLES FLICKERED TOO...

...AND YOU'RE FINALLY TAKING THE SUBJECT OF BATS SERIOUS, ARE YOU?
THIS IS SERIOUS, ARIANE.
AH.

MEANING CUT THE IRONY AND GET TO THE LORE--THE VERY SAME CURIOUS AND FORGOTTEN LORE I WAS PONDERING, IT JUST SO HAPPENS, WHEN YOU FLICKERED MY CANDLES WITH YOUR TYPICALLY MYSTERIOUS INVASION OF THE PREMISES.

YOU SEE?
COINCIDENCE?

DO YOU BELIEVE IN COINCIDENCE?
DO YOU BELIEVE IN VAMPIRES?
SURE--BUT ONLY BECAUSE IT'S NIGHT.
ASK ME IN THE MORNING...

HOW MIGHT THEY... COME TO BE?
HOW ARE VAMPIRES... CREATED?

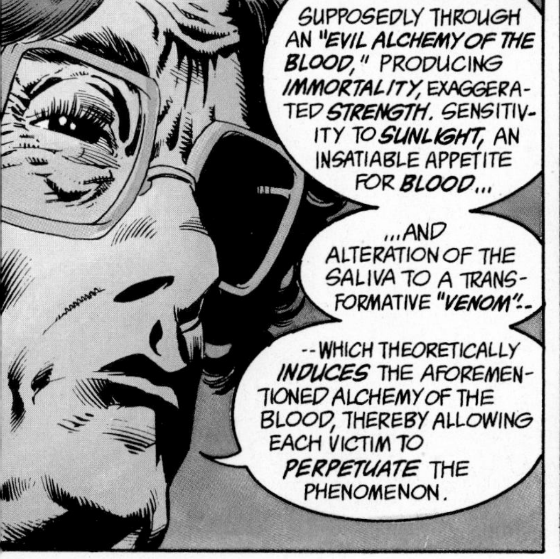
SUPPOSEDLY THROUGH AN "EVIL ALCHEMY OF THE BLOOD," PRODUCING IMMORTALITY, EXAGGERATED STRENGTH. SENSITIVITY TO SUNLIGHT, AN INSATIABLE APPETITE FOR BLOOD...
...AND ALTERATION OF THE SALIVA TO A TRANSFORMATIVE "VENOM"--
--WHICH THEORETICALLY INDUCES THE AFOREMENTIONED ALCHEMY OF THE BLOOD, THEREBY ALLOWING EACH VICTIM TO PERPETUATE THE PHENOMENON.

BY BITING NEW VICTIMS, LIKE IN THE MOVIES... AND LIKE THE TRANSFERENCE OF RABIES.
WHAT ELSE?
OH, THE USUAL.
THEY CAN TRANSFORM THEMSELVES INTO BATS, MIST, WOLVES... AND BE HARMED ONLY BY SILVER, THE CROSS, SUNLIGHT, DECAPITATION...

...AND, OF COURSE, THE EVER-RELIABLE OAK STAKE THROUGH THE HEART.
MUST A VAMPIRE BE... EVIL?
YOU MEAN, ASSUMING THEY REALLY EXIST?
ASSUMING THAT.
WELL, I DON'T KNOW...
THE RAIN IS TURNING REDDER, ISN'T IT? CHEMICALS IN THE AIR--ALCHEMY BY ACCIDENT --UNTIL SOON, THEY SAY, IT'LL STING THE EYES...
...BUT DOES THAT MAKE THE RAIN EVIL?
THE RAIN HAS NO WILL, ARIANE, NO CONSCIOUSNESS.
ALL RIGHT-- ARE PREDATORS EVIL?
AMONG BEASTS, PROBABLY NOT, BUT WE'RE ASSUMING VAMPIRES WERE ONCE HUMAN AND HUMANS HAVE THE CHOICE, FOR EXAMPLE, OF NOT HUNTING.
VEGETARIAN VAMPIRES.

A NOVEL NOTION, I'LL GIVE YOU THAT... BUT MAY I ASK WHY YOU'RE INQUIRING ON THE SUBJECT?
LET'S JUST SAY... TO ME, ALL CRIMINALS ARE "VAMPIRES" CLOAKED IN NIGHT TO PREY ON THE INNOCENT.
BUT RECENTLY...
YES?

NOTHING.
THANKS FOR YOUR EXPERTISE.
NOTHING YOU CAN'T FIND ON THE LATE SHOW.
BUT BY THE WAY, ARE YOU AWARE THAT TO SOME PEOPLE... YOU ARE NOT REAL?
TO OTHERS, YOU'RE VERY REAL... BUT ENTIRELY SUPERNATURAL...
THERE ARE EVEN THOSE WHO... WORSHIP YOU.
THERE ARE THOSE WHO WORSHIP MONEY, ARIANE, BUT IT SELDOM IMPROVES THEIR LIVES...
...NOR DOES THE MONEY CARE.
AMEN, BABY.
Potter's Field... where the city of Gotham provides simple graves for the destitute, the forgotten, the unknown...
Free dirt, for the poor.
But had they tried to claim it while living, they would have been arrested as thieves and trespassers.

As suspected, a number of the graves have been gutted...

But it had nothing to do with graverobbers-- and the victims number more than four.
Also as suspected, no one seems to have noticed the missing dead...
...but I wonder if all the crosses bothered them...as they trespassed on the way out.

The courtyard is still a dead-end.
I overlooked nothing.

No way out.
No possible means of escape--except as a bat...or...

...mist.
Nothing else could pass through this storm-grate...

RRRUNCHT
...not while its bars are cemented in stone.

Effortless again--sundered stone and all...

Lightning.

nd more ain.
Red rain...

Stinging.

KRUMP
Stone-rimmed steel bars...

and they reighed othing.
What is happening to me? And to Gotham?

Below...
The answers wait below--in Hell.

But it's far from hot.
A cold wet warren of suffocating stench...
Ripe, and rotting.
Death...

...stacked like cordwood--a lot more than four--and these are the ones who never reached Potter's Field... the ones who were spirited down here, either to die in filth or to be stored in it after death...
But... by whom?

SHFF
The pile trembles and lurches...

The movement comes from the bottom, from the oldest dead...
...squirming, now back to "life"...
...in hunger... in thirst...
...to find perfect prey, dropped right into their nest.
No telling how many there are...
...or when their "parents" might return.
Besides...
SWAKK
...I've gotten my answers.
TSH
TSH
TSH
But ahead--
PLASH
More of them.

Fresher ones.
Probably from Potter's Field...
...returned to life within their sealed coffins...

...and spared the decay of those incubated down here.
No choice now-- trapped between newborn behind me and seasoned predators ahead...

SHUMP

THRAKK

I've got to fight.

But even with my new strength...
...too many of them...
...and they're strong, too... overwhelming me...
Can't hold them off much longer...

HRAAHHH
...not when they're going--

HAUGH-K
CHUTCH

TO DEATH... IN PEACE.
TCHOK
TCHOK

CHUT
TUMPT

TO DEATH...
TCHOK
CHUTCH
...IN PEACE.
WH-WHO...?
VAMPIRES ARE REAL...

...BUT NOT ALL OF THEM... EVIL.
YOU--!
THE MIST...
BUT...

I AM TANYA-- AND YOU NEED NOT FEAR ME.
MY FOLLOWERS AND I ARE... THE OTHERS.
WE SEEK ONLY TO--

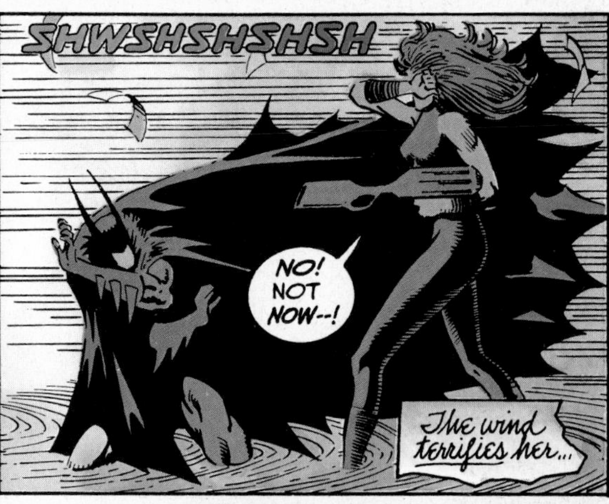
SHWSHSHSHSH
NO! NOT NOW--!
The wind terrifies her...

...fear borne on the vast, tattered wings of a monster.
AGAIN WE MEET, DEAR TANYA-- AND AGAIN YOU HUNT MY CHILDREN...

ON...
...YOUR...
...KNEES.
ALL OF YOU!

NOW--PUT AN END TO YOURSELVES!
Still groggy... weak...

Can't help her... not yet...

She's struggling against it... against his will, filling this foul chamber like a thick hypnotic haze...
They're all fighting it...

...but they're losing.

They can't hold out much longer
Got to gather my strength-- force myself to move... and--
DO IT!!

--break the spell.
GO, TANYA! GET OUT OF HERE!!
SHUMP
YOU DEFIED MEEEEE?!
Nothing left now... all fight gone...
Got to surrender to the filth...
...let myself float to the surface... and--
Blood.
SHRRRED
A single slash--bright red, whipping the air...

and he loves it.
JUST THE SIGHT OF IT... THE SCENT OF IT...
IT DRIVES YOU CRAZY, DOESN'T IT?
HRAAHHH
YOU WANT IT...
...COME AND GET IT...
HSSSSSSSS

Rage tightens him, quivering through his entire body.

He glares at the precious blood, shaped into exquisite pain. He can't stay away... can't come near.

A stalemate.

Silent hours pass, our eyes locked, blood pumping into a greasy link between us, farther tempting him from the filth.

Three times he licks his talons, the ones that ripped my chest... then licks his fangs.

L206
N-NOT EVEN...

...IF THERE'S ANY L-LEFT.

Even in daylight, it makes my blood run cold...
...even with the Mayor still playing it down, the news still ignoring it, the man on the street still chasing a buck on the way to his prime-time fix...
It stinks, even if I'm the only one who can smell it, even if my best homicide men dismiss it as a "kinky quirk" on the killer's part.

This isn't kinky; it's monstrous...
...and hardly the work of a "normal" serial killer.
Almost enough to make you believe in...
No. That way lies madness.

V-VAMPIRES, SIR? ARE YOU SURE YOU AREN'T--
DELIRIOUS, ALFRED...?

YES, I AM DELIRIOUS... DEFINITELY DELIRIOUS... BUT I'M NOT MISTAKEN.
VAMPIRES ARE REAL, AND--
SIR...!

YOUR... YOUR BACK, SIR!
I KNOW, ALFRED.
NOW... FINISH UP WITH THESE BANDAGES... AND JUST LET ME... REST.

"...IN PEACE..."
DESTROYED... ALL OF THEM... AND SHE'S GONE...
...SHE AND HER... "FOLLOWERS".

RULLUAAAHHH

ALL THAT TALK OF VAMPIRES... THE WAY HE'S ACTING...
AND HIS BACK...!
HE...HE'S CHANGING...

HE'S--
HIIIHH
LAST NIGHT'S RAIN...

TOO MUCH FOR THE FILTRATION SYSTEM TO HANDLE...

IT'S EVEN EATING AWAY AT THE ROOF NOW... A SLATE ROOF...

KILLING MORE TREES EVERY MONTH... DECREASING THE OXYGEN... FORCING SEAFOOD RESTAURANTS TO CLOSE...
ERAL
ATER

WHAT IS IT ALL DOING TO US?

ONE WAY OR ANOTHER, DIRECTLY OR NOT...
...IT'S CERTAINLY CHANGING WHAT WE DRINK.

PROBABLY CHANGING US, TOO.
LORD HELP US...
...WE'RE ALL CHANGING.

IT... IT'S NOT A DREAM... YOU'RE REALLY HERE... INSIDE MY BEDROOM...
YESSS.
T-TANYA...

YOU'VE PROGRESSED ENOUGH TO EXPERIENCE IT CONSCIOUSLY.
HARDLY... ANY BLOOD.
MY PURPOSE IS TO GIVE, NOT TAKE.
By avoiding the vein...

GIVE WHAT?
A GIFT YOU MAY COME TO NEED BEFORE THIS IS OVER.
BEFORE WHAT IS OVER?

THE HARVEST OF GOTHAM... BY THE LORD OF THE UNDEAD.

THEN IT WAS...
...DRACULA.

IT WAS NEVER BEFORE POSSIBLE FOR HIM TO PREY, UNDETECTED, ON SUCH A VAST SCALE -- BUT NOW, IN A LARGE MODERN CITY, WITH "NORMAL" BLOOD ATROCITIES SO PREVALENT, SO ACCEPTED, HORRIBLE DEATH AS A WAY OF LIFE, AND WITH SO MANY HOMELESS MAKING SUCH EASY VICTIMS...

NO ONE WILL EVEN MISS THOSE PEOPLE...
UNTIL IT'S TOO LATE -- UNTIL HIS LEGIONS HAVE GROWN LARGE ENOUGH TO START ON THE REST OF YOU.

AND YOU, TANYA... HOW DID YOU COME TO... OPPOSE HIM?
BY LOSING MY HUMANITY...
...AND BY JOURNEYING THROUGH HELL.

"HE TOOK ME ON AN AUTUMN NIGHT IN A TIME AND PLACE FAR FROM HERE AND NOW...
"...BLEEDING ME INTO THE HORROR OF HIS PRIVATE DARKNESS FOR WHAT PROMISED TO BE *FOREVER*.

"MY NEW LIFE, HOWEVER--A SEDUCTIVE, PRIMAL *PERVERSION* OF LIFE--ENDURED ONLY SOME SEVENTY YEARS... BUT IN THAT TIME, TO MY ETERNAL SHAME, I SHARED *MANY* LIVES WITH HIM...
"...LUSTING, ALWAYS, FOR *MORE*.

"IT WAS NOT UNTIL I FOUND HIM WITH A *CHILD* THAT I EVEN *REMEMBERED* MY FORMER LIFE...
"...*REAL* LIFE, SO VIVIDLY EMBODIED IN THAT FRESH, *INNOCENT* FORM...

"WITH THE FULL HORROR FINALLY *REALIZED*, HIS SPELL WAS *BROKEN*... LONG ENOUGH FOR ME TO ESCAPE HIS *WILL*.

"I FLED AS FAR AS I COULD, FEEDING ONLY ON *ANIMALS*...
"...EVEN THOUGH THE TASTE *SICKENED* ME, AND BARELY KEPT ME *ALIVE*.

"FINALLY, AFTER LOSING MYSELF, AND AFTER LONG YEARS OF WORK, ALL OF IT SELF-TAUGHT, I WAS ABLE TO DEVELOP A SERUM--AN ARTIFICIAL PLASMA, FOR WANT OF ANY BETTER TERM...
"...WITH WHICH TO WEAN MYSELF FROM THE HIDEOUS CYCLE OF PREYING AND KILLING AND CREATING EVER MORE OF THE UNDEAD.
"REAL BLOOD IS AN ADDICTION, AND IT WAS NOT EASY... BUT IN TIME AND AFTER GREAT AGONY I WAS FREED.
FROM THAT MOMENT ON I SOUGHT OUT OTHER VICTIMS OF HIS--OR HIS VICTIMS' VICTIMS--CONVINCING A FEW TO BECOME LIKE ME...
"...AND TO OPPOSE THEIR FORMER MASTER."
TOGETHER WE HAVE HUNTED DRACULA... FOR CENTURIES... NEVER EVEN GETTING CLOSE TO HIM... UNTIL NOW... HERE IN GOTHAM.
IT IS AS IF CAUTION AND ELUSIVENESS NO LONGER CONCERN HIM FOR SOME REASON--
--AS IF HE NO LONGER CARES ABOUT BEING CAUGHT...
AND YET, WHEN YOU DID CATCH HIM, DOWN IN THE SEWERS...
YES, IT WAS FUTILE... AS WE'VE KNOWN ALL ALONG IT WOULD BE.

THE BEST WE HAVE HOPED IS TO EITHER CONVERT EVER MORE OF HIS VICTIMS TO OUR CAUSE, OR TO SIMPLY LAY THEM TO REST.
AGAINST DRACULA HIMSELF, HOWEVER, WE ARE POWERLESS.

HAVING BEEN UNDER HIS SPELL, ALL OF US AT ONE TIME OR ANOTHER, WE CANNOT RESIST HIS ACTUAL PRESENCE... YET HE MUST BE STOPPED.
AND SO...
AND SO I'VE COME TO YOU... EVERY NIGHT FOR THE PAST MONTH.

AND NOW WE MUST SPEND THE REST OF THIS NIGHT MAKING PLANS--YOU AND I--FOR GOTHAM'S LAST BEST HOPE...

Morning, and she's gone again, just like all the other times... just like a dream...

...except it's not a dream... although definitely a nightmare.
If Tanya and her followers can't stop him... then maybe no one can.
But the plan's as good as it can be, and something must be done--Gotham must be warned.

Another day of rest... and then, tonight...
ALFRED!
I NEED YOU TO DELIVER A MESSAGE--TO GORDON!

SPARE CHANGE, FRIEND?
GO TO HELL, YOU LAZY LOUT!
NCIES
LABLE
Sign of the times. Back when, a bum might actually get invited in for a hot meal. These days he's an offensive nuisance, in the way at best, and maybe fit for nothing but death.

No, that's probably too cynical. Still, if nine out of ten people had their way, the homeless would at least disappear.
But why meet in this old section of town...?

And where the devil is--
OVER HERE, GORDON.
EH--?
THERE YOU ARE--AND WHY ALL THE MYSTERY?

WHY COULDN'T YOU MEET ME ON THE ROOF AS USU--
INSIDE, GORDON--AND YOU'LL SEE.

YOU SEEM WEAK... SICK OR HURT.
ARE YOU ALL RI--
YOUR CITY IS INFESTED WITH VAMPIRES, COMMISSIONER, FROM THE BOTTOM UP...
...AND YOUR CITY IS CRUMBLING OUT FROM UNDER YOU.
WHO THE--?!
YOU'RE LOOKING AT FRIENDS, GORDON, BUT YOU'RE ALSO LOOKING AT VAMPIRES.
VAMPIRES--? BUT... BUT THAT'S ABSURD!

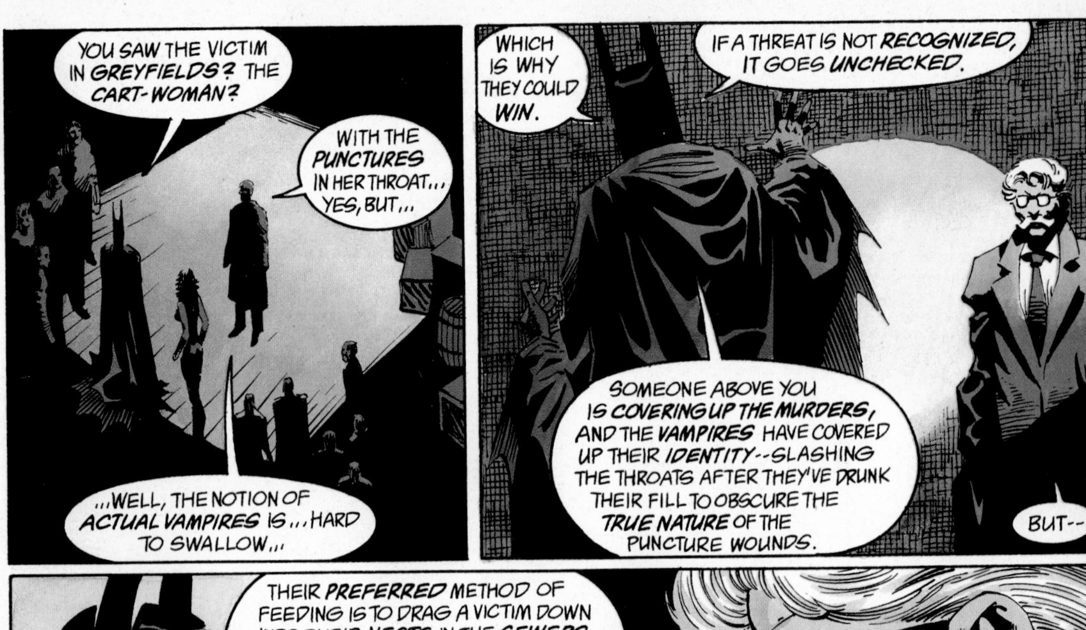
YOU SAW THE VICTIM IN GREYFIELDS? THE CART-WOMAN?
WITH THE PUNCTURES IN HER THROAT... YES, BUT...
...WELL, THE NOTION OF ACTUAL VAMPIRES IS... HARD TO SWALLOW...
WHICH IS WHY THEY COULD WIN.
IF A THREAT IS NOT RECOGNIZED, IT GOES UNCHECKED.
SOMEONE ABOVE YOU IS COVERING UP THE MURDERS, AND THE VAMPIRES HAVE COVERED UP THEIR IDENTITY--SLASHING THE THROATS AFTER THEY'VE DRUNK THEIR FILL TO OBSCURE THE TRUE NATURE OF THE PUNCTURE WOUNDS.
BUT--

THEIR PREFERRED METHOD OF FEEDING IS TO DRAG A VICTIM DOWN INTO THEIR NESTS IN THE SEWERS--BUT SOME GET DESPERATE OR GREEDY AND SIMPLY FEED ABOVE GROUND, PROVIDING YOUR UNDERESTIMATED AND COVERED-UP BODY COUNT.
I...
...I'M SORRY, BUT I... I JUST CAN'T BRING MYSELF TO BELIEVE IT...

THEN DRAW YOUR GUN, COMMISSIONER, AND SHOOT ME.
WH-WHAT?
YOU... YOU'RE CRAZY!
I CAN'T DO SOMETHING LIKE--

HREHRRRR

HSSSSSS
NO--!
BRAM BRAM BRAM
YOU SEE? HAD I REALLY WANTED YOUR BLOOD, COMMISSIONER...
...A THOUSAND BULLETS COULD NOT HAVE STOPPED ME.
AND YOUR CITY IS FACING DRACULA HIMSELF.
A-ALL RIGHT... IT... IT'S TRUE...AND THEY'RE STILL AT RISK... ALL THE ONES WE'VE CHOSEN NOT TO PROTECT...
EVENTUALLY, GORDON, WE'LL ALL BE AT RISK.
YES... BECAUSE WE'RE TURNING OUR BACKS NOW... LETTING IT SPREAD... AND THE MAYOR'S FEARS OF PANIC BE DAMNED.
I'LL BLOW IT WIDE OPEN, TELL THE WHOLE CITY... BUT YOU--? CAN YOU STOP HIM?
I DON'T KNOW.
HE HURT ME, GORDON... BADLY... AND I'M STILL TOO WEAK TO GO AT HIM AGAIN...

I NEED MORE REST... BUT IN THE MEANTIME, TANYA AND I HAVE A PLAN TO TAKE OUT THE REST OF THEM, IF NOT DRACULA HIMSELF.
WELL... JUST WATCH YOURSELF.
I'LL DO MY END OF IT WITH A PRESS CONFERENCE IN THE MORNING.

Minus the vampire angle, anyway.
That'll have to come later... broken gradually...

NOW, AS I SAID...
...THE MANOR... IS...
...L-LOCATED...

...UHNNN.
QUICKLY-- HELP HIM!
Vampires.
Even after watching her flesh fill three bullet holes before my eyes...
...it's still too unreal... a dark fantasy from some fever dream...

Graves... Emptied from within... cart-woman... stronger than ten men... stacked bodies... shifting... death squirming from the bottom of the pile... giant bat... his eyes... my back...
Woman's voice... Tanya?... speaking from a hollow distance... something about... "a disease of the blood"...
And now... a man's voice...
THE FEVER IS BREAKING, I THINK...
YES, HE'S REVIVING NOW.
WH-WHAT...?
THERE IS NO NEED FOR CONCERN. MY FOLLOWER IS -- WAS -- A DOCTOR
TRANS... FUSION...?
WE ARE THE SAME TYPE, YOU AND I.
TIME IS SHORT, AND YOU HAD LOST TOO MUCH BLOOD.
THERE WAS NO OTHER WAY.
AND... OUR PLAN...?

YOUR PEOPLE...WILL BE IN PLACE?
YES--AND NOW IT MUST WORK.
WHAT DO YOU--
WE LEAVE YOU NOW, BUT KNOW THAT DRACULA...HAS TAKEN YOUR FRIEND.
MY...FRIEND.
ALFRED!
BRACHT
ALLLLLFRED!!

GOOD LORD, SIR! WHAT--
ALFRED!
THANK GOD--SHE WAS WRONG...
I, AH, WAS JUST TAKING A CALL FROM DR. CHURCH, SIR...
BUT THEN... WHO DID SHE MEAN... IF YOU'RE...

IT SEEMS THE RESULTS OF YOUR BLOOD TESTS SHOW ABNORMAL LEVELS OF ADRENALINE...
...AS WELL AS AN INCREASED WHITE CELL COUNT, AND ANTIBODIES OF SOME UNKNOWN--

PEESH
BLASHH

SIR! WH-WHAT ON--
STAND BACK, ALFRED...
HRAAAH!

SWAKK
KILLING VAMPIRES GETS MESSY.

SHUMPT

THRAKK

SKRASH
The chair legs...
KRATCH
Four of them--
OH THAT DOPE!
--and only three vampires.
CHUTCH
More than enough.

V-VAMPIRES, SIR... BUT...I... I THOUGHT YOU WERE DELIRIOUS...
...AND AFTER DR. CHURCH'S CALL, I ASSUMED... JUST SOME... GOOD LORD... DISEASE OF THE B-BLOOD...
TANYA WAS STILL WRONG. SHE DIDN'T SAY HE WOULD TRY-- SHE SAID DRACULA HAD ALREADY TAKEN YOU...
DRACULA...?
KCY NEWS
--INTERRUPT NORMAL PROGRAMMING WITH THIS BULLETIN: POLICE COMMISSIONER JAMES GORDON IS MISSING AND FEARED ABDUCTED TONIGHT. WITNESSES DESCRIBE A TALL MAN WITH PIERCING EYES WHO--

GORDON!
MY "FRIEND"... NOT YOU, ALFRED... GORDON.
BUT... WHERE?
SIR, IF... IF THERE'S ANYTHING I CAN DO...

YOU KNOW WHAT TO DO, ALFRED-- WE CAN'T DROP THE PLAN NOW.
THE P-PLAN...? BUT SIR, I... I THOUGHT THAT WAS JUST YOUR DELIRIUM SPEA--
GOOD LORD, YOU WERE SERIOUS ABOUT IT.

WE... WE'RE REALLY GOING TO--
JUST GO, ALFRED! YOU KNOW WHERE TO MEET ME WHEN IT'S OVER.
Y-YES, SIR-- AND GOD SAVE COMMISSIONER GORDON.

NOT GOD, ALFRED...
ME.

"ARE YOU AWARE THAT GOTHAM'S BLOOD IS TAINTED?"
"YES--BY YOU."

NO, COMMISSIONER GORDON.
MY KISS ENRICHES THE BLOOD, CONFERRING STRENGTH AND IMMORTALITY.

THE FOULNESS OF WHICH I SPEAK IS YOUR OWN DOING...
...AND BELIEVE ME, I WOULD KNOW...
...HAVING BEEN A CONNOISSEUR FOR CENTURIES.
"CONNOISSEUR"--?

YOU'RE THE WORST ASS MURDERER OF THE AGES!
YES.
SO I AM... ALTHOUGH COMPETITION FROM YOUR RANKS HAS BEEN STEADILY GROWING.
BUT DO YOU KNOW WHAT HAPPENS TO BIRDS OF PREY FEEDING ON FISH FROM A POLLUTED STREAM?
SOMETIMES THEY DIE. SOMETIMES THEY MUTATE. AND SOMETIMES, COMMISSIONER GORDON...
...THEY GO MAD.

THAT WHICH AFFECTS THE PREY EVENTUALLY REACHES THE PREDATOR.
AND YOUR BLOOD, GORDON--THE BLOOD OF ALL HUMANS IN THIS MODERN WORLD--IS SLOWLY DRIVING ME MAD...
...JUST AS MAD, I'M AFRAID, AS YOUR HUMAN SOCIETY HAS BECOME.
YOU SEE, I NO LONGER CARE, GORDON ...AND THAT MAKES ME DANGER-OUS...
...MORE DANGEROUS THAN I HAVE EVER BEEN... MORE DANGEROUS THAN ANYONE OR ANYTHING COULD EVER BE.
GOTHAM HAS CHANGED ME, COMMISSIONER.
I HAVE BECOME...
...A TOTAL MONSTER.

AND YOU, COMMISSIONER... I HAVE CHOSEN YOU TO BEAR THE SINS OF THIS CITY...
MY VENGEANCE BEGINS WITH YOU--
--AND WITH YOUR FRIEND, WHEN HE ATTEMPTS TO RESCUE YOU...
.AND ONCE THAT VENGEANCE S COMPLETE, THIS HELL OF GOTHAM WILL BE MY HELL.
God help me... God give me strength.
MASTER'S GONNA HAVE BLUE BLOOD TONIGHT--COP BLUE--AND THEN THE COMMISSIONER CAN SOLVE HIS OWN MURDER FROM THE INSIDE. HYEE HEE HEE!
NO WAY THE MASTER WOULD BE THAT STUPID! HE'LL KILL GORDON...
..BUT HE ON'T TURN IM INTO A VAM--
CHTCH
CHAT
CHUT
HYEH.

BOO.
HIMMM...
GYYYET... HIM!
The darts drew blood but no pain...
We knew it would go down that way.
We counted on it.

They've got to chase me--all of them--and all the way to the end...
...all the way home.

Already they're hesitating, reluctant to leave their familiar maze of nests...
...unwilling to enter the unknown recesses of bypassed and abandoned tunnels...

But it's too late.
Tanya and her Others rise behind them, closing the merciful trap...
TCHOK
TCHOK
TCHOK
TCHOK
TO DEATH... IN PEACE.

CUTCH
AHRRR!
...herding them onward...
CHUT

...forcing them to follow me...
...ever deeper into the darkness...

...ever farther from Gotham's sewers and subways.
Only one last dead-end now, one final wall...
...but they've recovered my scent.
They're no longer fleeing Tanya...
They're pursuing me again.
DEET
No time to wait for the explosion to settle...
Got to crash the wall even as it disintegrates.
BAOUMM!
And the trap is now baited...

I'm home.
The vampires flood into the cave, Tanya and her Others close behind...
GO--INTO YOUR MANOR! WE'LL HOLD THEM!
As planned... and now the timing must be perfect...

Now the huge sacrifice Tanya and her Others have asked me to administer...must not be in vain.

The timing must be right...
It's got to be near dawn...

I timed the tunnel run three times when planting the explosives.
Let it work...
DEET
Let...there... be...

...light...
KUHKROOM
KRUMPHH!
...piercing the netherworld below.

Their cave breached, the bats will escape and flee-- but only the real ones, only the ones that will not burn in sunlight...
The others--all of them--are doomed.
FWHOOM
WHOOM
YAAAHH!
AAIEEE!
Not even one can be permitted escape...
YOU ARE THE LAST OF YOUR BRETHREN, UNHOLY ONE! OUT OF THE DARKNESS--NOW-- AND INTO THE LIGHT!
NO--AND NOR CAN YOU CROSS THE LIGHT, TANYA, TO REACH ME.
I CAN...
TSSSSSS
...AND I WILL...

AGH-K!
...FOR I NO LONGER FEAR THE LIGHT!
...IN PEACE...
FWHOOM
N-NO! N-NOT INTO IT... NOT IN--
TO DEATH--BOTH OF US...
WHOOM
...B-BLESSED...
...P-PEEEEACE--*

Trenchcoat and detonator.

If Tanya has succeeded, it's time now...

...time for one last gaze at my other home...

...because, now...
KTANK
KLATCH
TEK
DEET
BUHKROOOOOM!
...Wayne Manor is no more.

SHHROOOMMM!
And beneath its fall...
...so too falls the filling cave, my two homes become one tomb.
Full morning-- and its over.
Battered in my darkness, I can already hear the sirens' muffled moan and howl...
The plan has succeeded.
Dusk...
CAN'T GET OVER THE SIZE OF THE CAVE THAT WAS UNDER THIS PLACE -- MUST'VE BEEN A TREMOR-- JUST MADE THE WHOLE THING CAVE IN.
AND HOW.
WHOSE JOINT WAS THIS ANYWAY?
YOU DON'T KNOW--?

BRUCE WAYNE LIVED HERE--THE BIG-DEAL MULTI-MILLIONAIRE.
YEAH?
WELL, HIS DOUGH SURE CAN'T SAVE HIM NOW...

IF HE WAS HOME, HE'S THE LATE BRUCE WAYNE.
Dusk... and darkness...

It's safe, now, to rise.

My home... and the cave...
...everything they held...

...gone...

...crushed in a pit of blackness.
Memories... possessions... and most precious of all...

...a woman's ultimate courage.
GO--INTO YOUR MANOR! WE'LL HOLD THEM!

TO DEATH, TANYA...
...IN PEACE.

FWHHHHHHHHHHHHHHH!

SKREEEK

I KNOW, MONSTER.
IT'S FAR FROM OVER.

And the sky, torn by his passage, rains red again, gently now...
...but with all the promise of a fury yet and soon to come.

The heart of Gotham... the heart of the prize...

IT... IT'S OVER, SIR?
ALL BUT THE BIG ONE, ALFRED.

BUT HIS...HIS "FAMILY"?
AND THE MANOR?
I HEARD ON THE NEWS--
YES.
IT WAS THE ONLY WAY, ALFRED.

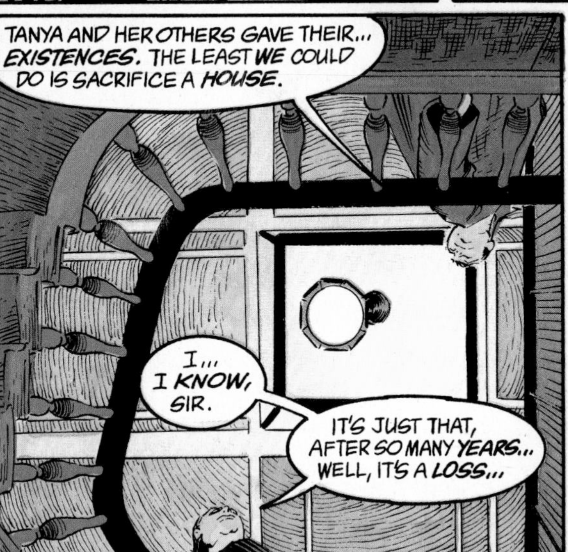
TANYA AND HER OTHERS GAVE THEIR... EXISTENCES. THE LEAST WE COULD DO IS SACRIFICE A HOUSE.
I... I KNOW, SIR.
IT'S JUST THAT, AFTER SO MANY YEARS... WELL, IT'S A LOSS...

FOR ME TOO, OLD FRIEND.
BUT WE'RE HARDLY HOMELESS.
YOU'VE DONE WELL IN PREPARING THIS BROWNSTONE, AND WE'LL BE MORE THAN COMFORTABLE-- RIGHT IN THE HUB OF THE CITY, CLOSE TO ALL THE ACTION...

...EQUIPPED WITH EVERYTHING WE NEED.

EXCEPT A CAVE, SIR... AND A GARAGE... NO PLACE FOR THE CAR.

FROM NOW ON, ALFRED--

--I WON'T BE NEEDING A CAR.
HIIIHH
GOOD...
...LORD!
A GREAT GIFT, ALFRED...
...FROM A GREAT AND HEROIC WOMAN.
TANYA IS DEAD, AT LAST... BUT HER LEGACY LIVES ON, IN ME...
"...TO BE BORNE THROUGH EVERY DARKNESS... ON THE WINDS."

A BAT-MAN, ALFRED, IN TRUTH NOW.
G-GO WITH GOD, SIR...
BUT YOU WILL NOT, FORGIVE ME, GO ALONE...
THE CAVE AND THE REAL CAR MAY BE LOST...
...BUT THERE'S STILL THE MERCEDES --MINUS THAT DOOR HANDLE ANYWAY.
First flight... final hunt.
And after the gauntlet hurled above the manor ruins... my quarry will hardly be hiding.
HE WILL FIND US SOON, GORDON, BUT I WONDER...
WILL YOU BE ALIVE... TO SEE HIS ARRIVAL?
ALIVE TO SEE HIS FALL?

WE SHALL SEE... BUT WHENEVER YOU DIE, GORDON--
--KNOW THAT ETERNAL LIFE WILL BE DENIED YOU.
YOUR BLOOD WILL BE MINE, YES, BUT MY KISS...
...WILL NOT BE YOURS.
AHNN--!
SHRAP
I AVOIDED THE VEIN, YOU SEE... AND YOURS WILL BE THE SLOW DEATH OF BLEEDING...
PLIP PLUP
...THEN... THE DARKNESS... FOREVER.
NO! THERE'S MORE THAN DARKNESS AT THE END!
BELIEVE YOUR FAIRY TALES IF IT COMFORTS YOU... BUT I HAVE BEEN THERE.
PLIP PLIP PLUP
TRUE DEATH IS NOTHING BUT DARKNESS, A VOID OF COLD BLACKNESS...
...UNTIL THE AWAKENING...
...AND FOR YOU... THERE SHALL BE NO AWAKENING.

...FORCING ME TO USURP HIS BROOD.
IT MUST BE OVER BETWEEN US--AND HE TOO MUST KNOW THE BLACKNESS...
PLIP PLUP PLIPT
YOU'RE MAD!
YOU SAID IT YOURSELF--HE'S COMING FOR ME!
PRECISELY WHY WE ARE HERE, COMMISSIONER. HE HAS ALREADY DESTROYED THE LARGEST FAMILY I HAVE EVER SPAWNED.
WORSE, HE MOCKED ME--TAUNTED ME--WITH HIS VERY BLOOD.
HE, TOO, MUST FEEL THE SLOW RAIN OF EBBING LIFE...
...UNTIL HE DROWNS IN THE VOID.
From the cave...
...from my cave...
EEE
SKEEE
...the bats...
...and they're his now.

SO HARD TO FOLLOW NOW THAT HE COMMANDS THE WHOLE SKY--
--AND ME CONFINED TO THE STREETS...

HONNK!
SKREEE
...BUT I'VE GOT TO KEEP HIM IN SIGHT!

--ANIMAL EXPERTS AND MUNICIPAL WORKERS NOW ATTEMPTING TO INV TIGATE THE HORDE OF APPARENTL BERSERK BATS SWARMING AROUND GOTHAM'S GAUDI BUILDING...
GFD
POLICE

"PRECISELY WHY THE FLYING CREATURES ARE ATTRACTED TO THIS LOCALE, NO ONE HAS YET BEEN ABLE TO SAY..."
SKREEEEE
LOOK OUT--!
MY GOD...!

"...BUT THE ATTRACTION HAS SWIFTLY AND REPEATEDLY PROVEN FATAL."

SO MUCH BLOOD...
...ALL WASTED.

SKEEEE
SKEEE
RABIES! A WHOLE COLONY OF RABID BATS!
GET BACK! STAY AWAY!!

SKEEE
SKEEE
SKEEE
PUT THE FIRE HOSES ON THEM!!
MARS
GAS 31¢
OIL
TIRES

WHAT THE--?!
WUD
FWUFF

SKEEE-EEE-EEE
PLUNCH

SKREEEE--
SKRASH!
GAS

Chaos...
...Gotham as Hell...
KEESH
FWAHROOM!
...all orchestrated from the central spire.
WHEN WILL HE COME, COMMISSION GORDON?
WHEN WILL YOUR DARK, AVENGING ANGEL--
KTANG!

NOW, DRACULA...
SILVER?
NOW!!
THRAKK

HRAHH
SHAP!

YOUR BLOOD, FOOL...
KISS IT GOODBYE.

He wants me to respond to the taunt.
And so I shall...

Big time.
Without words.
FWAKK
But his speed... his strength...
More than mine... far more...
GORDON...
TH-THANK GOD... YOU... YOU'RE HERE...

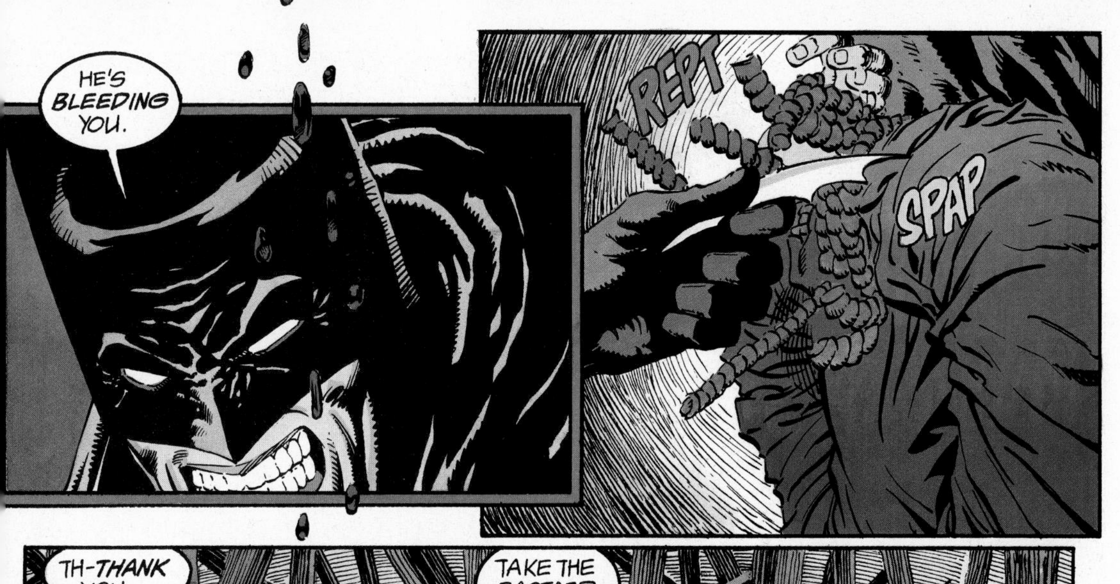
HE'S BLEEDING YOU.
REPT
SPAP

TH-THANK YOU...
NOW GET HIM, MAN...
TAKE THE BASTARD DOWN.

TANYA TRIED IT.
TANYA IS GONE.
BECAUSE OF ME, SHE LIVED FOR CENTURIES.
AFTER FINDING YOU, SHE DIED WITHIN WEEKS.
LIKE HER, YOU SHOULD HAVE FLED WHILE YOU HAD THE CHANCE.
SHE DIED BUILDING ME A BRIDGE TO YOU.
TO WHAT END? YOUR CITY IS MINE...
ITS PATHETIC HUMANS ARE MINE...
EVEN YOUR BATS ARE MINE...

LEAVING ME WITH NOTHING--
--BUT SILVER.

AAIIEEEE
CHTCH

SPLUNCHT

HYAHH!
HWOKK

FRAKK
Need distance...

...room to throw down.
IT HURTS, DOESN'T IT?

TSSS
TSS
SSS
YAHRRR!

BURNS LIKE HELL.
TWO CAN BLEED, DRACULA-- AND MY SILVER MAKES YOUR BLOOD BOIL.

CHTCH
CHT
SHEKT

YEEEAHRRRRRRR
He's trying to escape--leaping into the night, into the lightning and red rain...

...shedding the silver...
...thinking he's safe now...
...sole master of the raging sky.

He's wrong.
NOOOOO!!

As is Gordon.
W-WINGS?

NIGHTMARE ... AN ABSOLUTE NIGHTMARE.
TWO GREAT MONSTERS FLAPPING THROUGH THE STORM.

... LEAVING THE CITY NOW... TO COME AGROUND GOD ONLY KNOWS WHERE.
Got to overtake him -- before he knows I'm coming.
More, got to rise above him -- for the kill...

Now.

FWWWUFFT

YOU--!
TANYA DID THIS--
GAVE YOU NEW
FORM...

...YET SHE LET YOU LIVE!
His strength is.. impossible...
SHE WAS MEANT TO TAKE-- NOT GIVE!
He's beating me away--as if I were no more than a sparrow.
TAKE YOUR BLOOD--TAKE YOUR LIFE!
SHKCH
AHRRR!

His fangs are like fire in my flesh--this mouth a foul wet thing of cruel greed...
...working urgently at my throat... sucking to the rhythm of my pulse...
Vision dimming... losing it... got to "bite" back...

SHRAAK
BRATCH
FZZZT
FZZZT
...with silver.

THTCH
YEEAHRRR!

Below...

The lightning-- bearing a gift from the heavens...

Got to force him down while he's still in pain--then kick free at the last moment...
...so that I...

SHUKT
REEEEEEAAAIIIEEEEEEEEE
--am not impaled...
...through the heart...
...on a stake of dead oak.
His shriek... cutting through the thunder... a wail of agony and loss that could only be voiced by one who has lived so long... and has wielded a power beyond the world's measure...

He chokes, on the blood of thousands... smoldering now...
FHWOOOM
...becoming a raft of hell's flame here on earth.
Ariane was right... and so was Tanya.
Vampires are real...
...and while some are merely predators...
...and a precious few are actually noble...
...Dracula himself was wickedness incarnate.

But he's gone now...
The lord of depravity is dead... his ashes a sodden stench under the red rain...
...while I... dizzy... so hard to rise... to remain standing...
He took... so much blood... and... I'm bleeding still...
I...

I think...
...I'm...
...dying.

SKREEETCH

MASTER BRUCE--!!

NO...
OH, NO...
NO, NO, NO, NO...
NOOOOOOOOOOOOO

SEVEN DAYS LATER...
BUT IT WASN'T JUST YOU-- WE ALL WANTED TO IGNORE IT...
...AND WITH FEDERAL FUNDS FOR HOUSING SLASHED TO THE BONE AND BLED DRY...

...YOU CAN'T BLAME YOURSEL--
THE PROTEST IS APPRECIATED, COMMISSIONER GORDON, BUT THE HONORABLE THING IS PAST DUE.
I ONLY HOPE MY EXAMPLE SERVES THE NEXT ADMINISTRATION.
GOTHAM

LADIES AND GENTLEMEN, EFFECTIVE IMMEDIATELY, I RESIGN THE OFFICE OF MAYOR OF THE CITY OF GOTHAM.
WHAAAT?!

MY FINAL OFFICIAL ACT, THIS MORNING, INSTRUCTED THE DISTRICT ATTORNEY TO ARRAIGN ME ON CHARGES OF CRIMINAL NEGLECT...
And in leaving us, he becomes precisely the man we need...

...especially now.
MASTER BRUCE... I TRIED TO SERVE YOU...
...AS BEST I COULD...
...WHETHER ASKED OR UNBIDDEN...
WAYNE

BUT IN THE END...
...IT WAS YOUR SERVICE...
...WHICH SAVED US ALL.

THE WORLD SHALL NEVER AGAIN KNOW YOUR MEASURE.
FAREWELL... SIR.
BRUCE WAYNE

"--HEREWITH APPOINT ALFRED PENNYWORTH SOLE EXECUTOR OF THE WAYNE FORTUNE...
"...NINE-TENTHS OF WHICH SHALL BE ADMINISTERED THROUGH A NEW FOUNDATION TO BE NAMED "HOUSING FOR THE HOMELESS"...

I'M, AH, ALREADY AWARE OF ALL THIS...
"OF MY REMAINING ASSETS AND ESTATES...

IT WAS PART OF... THE PLAN.
"...AS DETAILED IN ATTACHMENT-C..."
SO... I'LL BE LEAVING NOW.

NO MANOR... NO CAVE... BUT "WE'LL BE MORE THAN COMFORTABLE," HE SAID...
VACANCIES AVAILABLE

"...RIGHT IN THE HUB OF THE CITY... WITH EVERYTHING WE NEED."

I... STILL CAN'T GET OVER IT, SIR.
WHEN I FOUND YOU...
...THERE WASN'T THE LEAST SPARK OF LIFE.
I COULD HAVE SWORN YOU WERE ACTUALLY--
I AM DEAD, ALFRED.
S-SIR--?
BUT DON'T WORRY.
BRUCE WAYNE MAY BE GONE...
...BUT THE BATMAN WILL GO ON...
...FOREVER.
Vampires are real...
...but not all of them... evil.